WE LOVE LUCY

NEW LOVERS is a series devoted to
publishing new works of erotica
that explore the complexities
bedevilling contemporary
life, culture, and
art today.

WE LOVE LUCY

×

LILITH WES

BADLANDS UNLIMITED
NEW LOVERS
Nº2

We Love Lucy
by Lilith Wes

New Lovers No.2

Published by:
Badlands Unlimited
P.O. Box 320310
Brooklyn, NY 11232
Tel: +1 718 788 6668
operator@badlandsunlimited.com
www.badlandsunlimited.com

Series editors: Paul Chan, Ian Cheng, Micaela Durand, Matthew So
Consulting editor: Karen Marta
Copy editor: Charlotte Carter
Editorial assistant: Jessica Jackson
Ebook designer: Ian Cheng
Front cover design by Kobi Benzari
Endpaper art by Paul Chan
Special thanks to Luke Brown, Alex Galan, Martha Fleming-Ives, Elisa
Leshowitz, Marlo Poras, Cassie Raihl, David Torrone

Paper book distributed in the Americas by:
ARTBOOK | D.A.P. USA
155 6th Avenue, 2nd Floor
New York, NY 10013
Tel. +1 800 338 BOOK
www.artbook.com

Paper book distributed in Europe by:
Buchhandlung Walther König
Ehrenstrasse 4
50672 Köln
www.buchhandlung-walther-koenig.de

Printed in the United States of America

ISBN: 978-1-936440-82-5
E-Book ISBN: 978-1-936440-83-2

www.badlandsunlimited.com

CONTENTS

Chapter 1

Nicholas was the only gay man I'd ever fallen in love with. The beginning of our friendship was simple and random. I'd left my apartment one morning after running out of coffee the previous day and gone down to the cafe on the corner for my morning fix. The wait was long and every table was full, but there was one empty chair opposite an attractive young man in the corner. I shuffled through, careful not to spill the boiling hot beverage on myself, before I stood bleary-eyed at the edge of his table.

"Would you mind?" I asked while pulling back the chair, inadvertently releasing a high pitched squeal as it scraped across the tile floor.

He looked up briefly, a small, quick smile on his full lips. "No, not at all," he said pleasantly before he went back to his book, leaving me to sit in peace.

We were twenty-three then; and now, seven years later, I was waiting at home for him and his boyfriend, James, to arrive. It was my thirtieth birthday and they had promised a night of dinner and dancing at our favorite club. "A night of debauchery and hedonism" had been Nicholas's exact words, and I was particularly looking forward to it.

In reality, I wasn't in love with him anymore; he had become my best friend. I had relied on him more than once over the past several years, through the slew of boyfriends and one-night stands, the job changes, and the unexpected passing of my father last year. He had been through it all with me, and now James had too; they are my surrogate husbands. I have other friends, girlfriends, and a few other male acquaintances, but Nicholas and James are where my heart lies, for now anyway. My last relationship ended a few months ago and I can't say that I was very upset. He was fine for a while, kind, with a sense of humor; but he was soft and relenting—and that wasn't what I wanted. I knew what I wanted and I was happy to keep looking for it.

I checked my phone for the time. *They should be here soon,* I thought, heading to the bathroom for one last check on the hair. It was behaving; long and loose like I normally wear it, the soft brown ends resting between my shoulder blades. The sheer black fitted blouse hugged my small breasts and tapered down over the ample hips that are my birthright. I had overdone it on the black eyeliner and mascara, but we were going to the club and there was no other way to make my pale features noticeable in the darkness of the dance floor. I had every intention of finding my own birthday present before the night was through. The bell drew me out to the door, and the approval on their faces was apparent as it swung wide.

"You look hot," Nicholas said, coming

in with his arms full of assorted bags. "I'm glad I made you buy that skirt. Every straight man will be staring at your ass tonight." He laughed, leaning in and giving me a kiss on the mouth, as was our traditional greeting, but tonight it felt different. I looked up at James as my fingers ran over the remnants of his touch to find his brown eyes intent on my green ones, the corners of his mouth pulled in an upward consent.

"Happy birthday, Lucy," he said before kissing me in the same manner Nicholas had.

"I'll bet it won't be just straight men admiring your ass tonight," he whispered flirtatiously in my ear as he pulled away with a smirk. James was dressed in his usual manner, a black v-neck t-shirt and snug- fitting overpriced designer jeans, but it looked like Nick had intervened by putting a dark purple button-up shirt over the ensemble for our night out. My eyes lingered on his retreating figure, his long, lean muscular build concealing Nicholas's smaller frame in front of him as they entered the kitchen. Both men set their bags on the counter before turning back to me.

"You can shut the door, Lucy," Nick said, grinning. "We decided to make you dinner instead."

"Great," I replied. "Then out to the club, I take it?"

They looked at each other before James answered slyly. "That is, of course, if we get there."

"Sorry, but has the entire evening been readjusted?" I asked, slightly confused.

"Only if you want it to be," Nick said.

"It is your birthday, after all."

Just the way he said it made me laugh. "You two are up to no good." I pointed at them. "Well, what is this new plan? Stay in and have a wake for the old lady?"

"Hey, wait! *I'll* be thirty next month," Nicholas said. "Thirty's not old, we're just getting started, love." He cracked the seal on a bottle of vodka that had suddenly appeared from one of the bags. "Let me get you a drink and we can talk about it."

I sat watching them hum around the small white box of a kitchen. Ice and a slice of lemon went into the glass before the vodka as Nicholas intermittently looked over at me to gauge how I was taking this turn of events, but I was used to it. He was famous for his spontaneity and it was one of the many reasons

James and I loved him; he was the singular creature who kept us from the monotony of our lives.

Nicholas crossed the small room and sat next to me on the red velvet sofa, my prized possession. I had bought it with several years of saved Christmas money. I felt the slip of the cold glass in my hand and immediately took a sip as Nick nervously ran his hand through his light brown hair. He paused before speaking, pulling at the cuff of his shirt until it was adjusted to the perfect placement at the end of his wrist. Nicholas was always impeccably groomed and tonight was no exception. The slate grey shirt was snug, highlighting the muscular triangle of an upper body he referred to as his "Louganis"—due to his childhood crush—and his black jeans screamed of a price tag in the neighborhood of my rent check. He was, as always, the most beautiful boy I'd ever seen, regardless of what he was wearing.

"Last night we were talking," he said, finally looking over at James, who had placed himself opposite us in the green chair reclaimed from the street, his long legs spread wide. "And we wanted to give you something special for such a milestone birthday."

"Milestone?" I choked as the vodka burned down my throat.

James chuckled. "Again, this is my fault. I made the suggestion, so all the blame can be thrown my way."

I glanced back at Nick. "Look, I'm not mad. In fact, I don't really care what we do. It's just a birthday, and not a very big one at that, right? We're still young and handsome," I joked, nudging him and taking another sip.

"Exactly my point last night," James interjected, his face serious as he leaned forward. "I suggested to Nick that we should give you something lasting, something I think you would perhaps enjoy very much. It took some convincing, but I think Nicholas has come around quite well to the idea."

Nick blushed fully, even the tips of his ears reddening. "What my ever-so-clever boy is saying is that we want you to watch."

"Watch what? TV, a movie, ping-pong? Just tell me," I said, getting slightly irritated at the go round they were putting me through.

"Us. We want you to watch us," James said. "Will you, Lucy?"

The burn of his eyes told me everything I needed to know, and the flutter that rolled through my stomach and into my groin gave me my answer.

"You want me to watch you two have sex? That is my present?"

"Look, it was a silly idea, wasn't it, James?" Nicholas said suddenly as he stood up, glaring at his partner. "I need a drink."

"Wait, sit back down, please." I motioned to the empty space beside me. As he eased into the warm velvet, I took another long sip. "So, this was your idea?" I asked, looking accusingly at James.

"Yes, and in case you were unaware, I am a bit of an exhibitionist, to which Nick can attest most adamantly." He was looking hard at Nicholas now, eyes dark as the idea of fucking him in front of me started to take on a more realistic shape.

"Nick told me a long time ago that you had a fantasy about watching two men have sex together, so what better gift could we give you than making a fantasy come true?"

The drink was gone now, the ice clicking against my teeth, but I didn't remember taking that last long swallow. My mind was too busy thinking about how this would work and if I could actually stand to be in the same room with them fully engaged without wanting to join in. It had, of course, crossed my mind on occasion, and how could it not? They were extremely affectionate with each other no matter where we happened to be, and sometimes it spilled over onto me. It was always welcome, but it held a promise that was never fulfilled, until now.

"Yes," I said, looking directly at James.

"Excellent," was the only word he uttered before rising slowly from the chair and extending his hand to Nick.

"You're sure?" Nicholas asked, ignoring the gesture.

"Yes, again," I whispered, kissing him fully on the mouth, now completely turned on at the thought of their forthcoming exhibition. "Thank you for such a generous gift."

He grinned and ran the slight stubble of his check across mine until his lips were at my ear. "You won't be disappointed, James has a beautiful cock," he whispered, making me laugh.

"I know, love, you've told me a million times," came my retort as our foreheads met in solidarity.

James cleared his throat, turning Nick's attention back to him.

"Shall we get started?"

"What about dinner?" Nick asked.

James looked over at me. "I think Lucy is more than ready to receive her present and I would find it difficult myself to wait now that we are all agreed."

I nodded my head as James pulled Nicholas towards the bedroom. "I'll just get myself another drink then."

"Bring the bottle," Nick called out as he disappeared into the dark room.

I took my time, even prepared two more glasses, allowing them the opportunity to move past the initial awkward stage of having me watch from the very beginning.

The only light that brightened the small cramped bedroom came from the streetlight outside illuminating the two nude bodies that were already intertwined on the bed. I set the three glasses on my dresser, seemingly undetected, and poured them full as the low sounds of sucking and intermittent moans filtered into my ears. The floor seemed the best place to remain as unobtrusive as possible, so I settled in, slowly sipping the cold vodka. It did little to brace me for what I was seeing.

A moment later the two men rose onto their knees, still touching, their hard cocks slicing against each other as they kissed sensuously.

Nicholas turned his head towards me, breaking the kiss. "Can you see well enough, Lucy?" he asked as James grabbed his cock and began to stroke him.

"Yes, very well now," I said, keeping

my voice low, afraid to break the mood.

James chuckled and pulled Nick's head around to claim his lips again. They were beautiful, more so than I ever could have imagined; their bodies coming in and out of contact in an almost combative way, tempered only by the erotic moans that escaped their fully occupied mouths.

James left Nicholas's lips with purpose and began to suck on his dark brown nipples. Nick threaded his fingers through the lush black hair that graced his lover's crown and gave him a soft command that I couldn't hear but immediately understood. Nick let himself fall back on the bed and stretched his long legs on either side of James as his hand wrapped around the base of his own shaft. James gave the thick cock a demanding slap before leaning forward and taking him entirely in his mouth, making Nick's hips thrust at the sensation.

I was wet, wetter than I had been in a very long time, my carefully chosen "fuck me" birthday underwear soaked through long before I thought it would be tonight. As Nicholas writhed under James, I leaned forward, my eyes unable to tear themselves away from the erotic bliss before me.

The last five minutes of our seasoned friendship was the most alluring it had ever been. And then it changed forever.

Chapter 2

I heard my name, but it didn't register at first. I was wholly intent on watching James, his rhythm slow and powerful as he drew Nick's cock between his lips.

"Lucy," Nicholas said again, this time with more urgency.

My eyes went up his prone body until I saw the silhouette of his raised head.

"Yes, what?" I snipped, not wanting

to be distracted.

"Bring me a drink, love," he said, the last word coming out as a groan.

I found it hard to move, especially as James was becoming more pressing in his desire to pleasure the exquisite male beneath him. As I uncrossed my legs, I became painfully aware of how excited their exhibition had made me. I brushed my hand across the back of my skirt as I rose, just to make sure the wetness hadn't soaked thorough.

Retrieving the vodka, I made my way over to the bed, trying to keep my eyes locked on Nick's contorted face. "Here," I whispered, unable to keep from glancing downward.

Nicholas raised up onto his elbows and took the glass, making James pause.

"May I have a sip too?" James rubbed

his stubbly cheek over the spit-soaked shaft in front him. Nicholas sat up and placed the glass to his lips and allowed him a drink.

"Sit, will you?" Nick asked, looking up at me.

"Where? On the bed?"

James pulled back and wiped the cold liquid off his lips, a sly smirk appearing as his hand crossed his face. "Yes, of course. Where else?"

His large brown eyes were almost completely concealed by his disheveled thick dark hair and I had the sudden urge to lean over and kiss him, but I resisted and did as I was asked. I eased down, allowing myself only a small space, one ass cheek hanging off the side of the mattress.

Nick took a long drink and set the vodka on the floor, his cold hand running up my leg before he rolled over onto his stomach. "I want you here, beside me, when James fucks me."

My breath caught audibly in my throat. I had been more than happy to remain where I was, but it seemed they wanted to share more with me then they had let on.

Nicholas rose to his hands and knees, giving James the opportunity to rim him, but my attention now was on Nick's face, the pleasure of James's ministrations causing the full gambit of emotions to run across his striking features. His eyes opened slowly, finding mine in the dimness of the room.

"Kiss me," he demanded with a desperate edge to his voice.

I must have pulled back, because I lost my balance and almost landed on the floor, making Nick snort. "Sorry, what did you say?" I asked, righting myself.

"Kiss me, Lucy, just this once. Kiss me like we are in love."

My heart started to pound and I could feel a surge of wetness between my legs. I looked back at James, trying to gauge his reaction to Nick's request.

On cue, he rose from behind his lover, speaking what he knew I needed to hear.

"Go ahead, kiss him. You have my permission." He smiled before edging forward, pressing his thick cock between the valley of Nick's ass cheeks.

Nicholas groaned and slid his hand across the sheets until it found mine.

"Come here," he whispered. I inched forward, awkward at first, but the look he gave me urged me to comply. I leaned in, my hand still under his, and gave him the most sensuous kiss I could. A low noise came from deep in his chest as he answered my softness with something I had never felt from him. He was almost brutal, his tongue running the crease of my lips, trying to slip its way inside, and I finally let him.

In the next minute I was kissing him like I had wanted to all those years ago, my hands on either side of his face, pulling him into me as hard as I could. I was lost momentarily, the lust making me grind my ass into the bed. He stopped when he felt me move, his lips forming a smile against mine.

Nick rose, an urgency filling his voice. "Get up here, on your knees," he ordered.

I obeyed, glancing at James, who was now rolling on a condom. Face-to-face with my friend, I leaned in as he ran a hand up the back of my neck and began to kiss me again. His other hand pushed its way underneath the bottom edge of my blouse, fingers splayed wide as he roamed over the soft flesh of my belly.

"You have too many clothes on," he said, using both hands to reveal me in one quick upward tug.

"Take her bra off," James said, looking over Nick's shoulder, his fingers digging into the slim hip as the other hand stroked the long cock in front of me.

I reached around and undid the clasp, but didn't pull it off. I was fully engaged now, my lust running down the inside of my thighs.

Nick eased the straps down my arms, revealing my small, upturned breasts, and threw the bra on the floor.

"Hmmm, those are quite lovely,"

came James's heavy voice in the dark. "I want you to suck her, Nick. Take one of those little pink nipples in your mouth and suck while I fuck you."

Nicholas complied immediately. He glanced up at me only once before his hands slipped down the back of my skirt to grab a handful of ass. My eyes closed as his hot mouth pulled the nub between his lips, his teeth biting down in a pleasant manner. I ran my hands through his hair as I watched James slowly push himself inside. Nick hissed at the intrusion and moved back to my mouth. The kiss was hard, his mouth and body bumping against mine as James started to move.

Inadvertently my hand moved to the cock against my belly. "Is this all right?" I asked stroking him gently.

"Fuck yes," he bit out, tugging me forward.

James was just inches from my face now, eyes hooded as he moved inside Nicholas's tight ass.

"How wet are you, Lucy?" he asked, his tongue snaking up his lover's taut neck before biting down on the earlobe. "If I tell Nick to put his hand down your panties and rub your clit, will you come?"

"Yes," I moaned, realizing who was, in fact, driving this show. "Do you want Nick to fuck me?" I blurted out, not caring what the repercussions would be when this was all over.

James raised his brow. "See, I told you she wanted to. She's wanted to fuck you for a long time. Haven't you, Lucy?" He plowed into Nick harder, pushing his swollen cock into my lower belly.

I don't know what made me say it, but it seemed the obvious answer to his question in that moment. "Yes, but I want you to fuck me too, James."

Nicholas groaned and pulled my skirt down over my hips in one powerful tug. "Take these off," he ordered, sliding a warm hand under the waistband of my panties. "Oh my god, you are so fucking wet," he said in amazement as his finger ran down my slit.

My hips bucked against his tentative exploration, the thought of whose hand was rubbing my cunt making me shudder. I took his mouth again as James watched with approval, his thrusts slowing down as my hand sped up on Nick's shaft.

"I think we need another condom," James said in an amused tone as he pulled out and reached for his discarded jeans.

Nick took the opportunity and pulled back, whispering, "Are you sure you're okay with this?"

"I'm very okay with it. Are you?"

Nick ran his finger up and down my slit until he found the hard nub, making me pant with consent. "Here? Is this right? I rub this while I'm fucking you?" he asked as my legs shook.

"Yes, please, Nick," I moaned. "You're going to make me come."

"Really? I've never made a woman come before, but if I do, it should be you, shouldn't it?" The awareness of what we were about to do was evident both in the look we gave each other and the softness compressing the end of his question.

I felt James press Nick into me again, the moment passing. "Here," he said, handing me the condom.

I ripped the foil and rolled it over the hard cock in front of me. Once I was finished, I stood and removed the rest of my clothes, watching as James pushed himself back into Nicholas with one slow thrust. There was a moment of hesitation on my part as I wondered what to do next, but James took charge.

"Get on your knees in front of him," he said, noting my delay.

I leaned over and kissed Nick first before maneuvering myself as gracefully as possible to where I needed to be. As soon as I was close, he impatiently grabbed my hips and pulled, sliding me towards his twitching cock.

"Fuck," he sighed as his cock ran the length of my slit.

I reached back and guided him to where I wanted him, my legs trembling as I pushed my body back against his. I heard him inhale sharply once he was completely inside.

The hard thrusts from James were the only movement for a long minute as Nicholas massaged the thickness of my ass and hips. Very gently I began to rock, feeling both full and strangely empty at the same time.

"Wait, wait, James, stop," he cried as his fingertips dug into the flesh of my body.

"What's wrong?" James asked, coming to a halt.

"Nothing is wrong. I just, I just feel a little overwhelmed." He panted, grinding against me.

There was a low chuckle that I felt more that heard. "You have a beautiful cock buried in your ass and yours is buried inside a beautiful woman. Of course you are overwhelmed."

Nicholas sighed. "God, I love you, James." He exhaled and turned to give him a long kiss. As he started moving inside me again, his one hand left my hip and ran over my flushed skin until he reached my cunt. He leaned forward until his front was against my back. "Does that feel good?" he asked, rubbing my clit as he fucked me.

"Yes, god, yes," I panted as my strength left me, my upper body collapsing on the bed. And all I could feel was him. I could tell the moment James started moving again. Nicholas had been thrusting into me at a gentle pace, but as soon as James renewed his efforts, Nick drove into me with purpose.

For a second I thought I would come, but James turned the tables on me again. He pushed against Nick, bending him forward until we three were pressed together. It was then I felt another hand run down the inside of my thigh.

"She's soaking wet, Nick. We did that to her, just watching us." His voice trailed off as his fingers ran down the side of my outer lips, coating themselves in my arousal. "Fuck," James cursed as he began plowing into Nick at a furious pace. Nicholas righted himself and began to fuck me harder, his fingers leaving my clit in order for him to hold on to my hips for leverage.

My nipples scraped across the sheets, creating a delightful friction in addition to the hard cock pounding away inside my soaking wet cunt. A minute later I was coming.

Chapter 3

The sound of my own release was strange and implausible, an animalistic cry that reverberated the whole way to my groin. As soon as my orgasm began, Nick started fucking me so hard I was sure I was going to have a burn from the comforter on my face in the morning. He groaned something and drove into my aching cunt like he had been fucking women his whole life. It felt so good, the power of his cock inside me, the slap of his balls on the underside of my cunt. I could tell he was going to come soon.

I pushed myself up on my hands and looked back at them. James too was nearing the edge as he clenched his lover's shoulder, the redness spreading out across Nick's skin from the pressure. Nick's eyes were closed, his face twisted in pleasure as his own orgasm came to a head.

"Jesus," he spat, his body halfway between limp and pained as he came with James still pounding into him from behind, the sweat from James's brow dripping onto his back.

James let go of his shoulder and pushed Nick forward until he was bent over against me. I could still feel his hard cock inside, moving with each trust of

James's hips.

I craned my head back, trying to kiss Nicholas, but it was he who ran his free hand under my throat and brought my lips to his. The tenderness was disarming, the cut of his kiss making me squirm in agony. James started whispering behind us. "Yes, just like that," he chanted as we became more disconnected from the world. Suddenly I felt another orgasm building, but James was finished, his movements slowing incrementally inside his lover. Moments later it was over.

"You were so gorgeous, Lucy," Nicholas murmured as he pulled out and away, back to the one he belonged to.

I watched unwillingly as James ran his hands up and down Nick's slick chest before he disengaged. "That was incredible," he whispered just before claiming Nick's lips in a way that I cannot describe. It was beautiful and tender, the possession it declared unmistakable.

"I'll be right back," he said, giving me a long look before he went into the bathroom. Nicolas laid down and pulled me into him, his hands running over my hot skin.

"Did you like your present?" he asked so innocently it almost broke my heart.

"Yes, very much," I sighed, then grabbed his hand and brought it to my lips for a kiss. "Best present I ever got."

Nick laughed. "Really? The best ever?"

"Ass, you know it was. You know everything about me," I stated with certainty. "How was your first time ever with a woman?" I countered, feeling a little uncomfortable.

"Best first time with a woman EVER,"

came the reply, topped with a bite to my neck.

"And last, I suppose. Well, at least you had one of the finest," I said, tucking myself further into the hard body behind me.

"True. Well, that's what I've heard anyway."

I chuckled softly. "I'll be sure to remind you of that on a regular basis," I said. James came back into the room and stood at the edge of the bed in front of me, his cock still partially hard. When I looked up at him, his eyes were focused behind me, his face unreadable. I watched as he nudged Nicholas off the bed with nothing more than a nod of his head towards the bathroom. As the heat from behind me retreated, it was replaced by a more intense warmth, one that did nothing but make my stomach flutter with anticipation.

James ran his hand down over my shoulder and back before coming to rest on my ass. He pulled me tight against him.

"Was that to your satisfaction?" he asked, staring into my eyes.

"Yes, thank you."

"I watched you orgasm, Lucy. I thought at one point the force of your hips was going to push me off the bed."

I chuckled and broke the stare. "That bad, was it?"

"No, it was quite beautiful," he said seriously. "But I think it's my turn now."

I looked back into his eyes, afraid I had asked for much more than I was able to handle. "I didn't mean, I mean, you don't have to," I stuttered, instantly feeling that swell between my legs.

James chuckled and ran his hand

down my belly towards my cunt. "Oh, I want to and you want me to."

"But you already came," I blurted out as his finger found my clit. Groaning, I pushed against his hand. "You can't come again, can you?"

"Hasn't Nick told you about my stamina yet?" he asked, sounding disappointed. "I'll have to punish him." He smiled, rubbing me faster.

My mouth was open in a pant and I could hardly find the words to answer him as he stroked me with an expertise that was unfamiliar.

"Yes, but I seriously thought he was lying," I uttered before trying to wiggle away from his quickening touch.

"No, no, stay right where you are." His free hand went to the back of my neck and held me in place. "You are going to come for me now."

James placed his forehead gently against mine while he slipped two fingers inside my already soaked cunt. His thumb came back to my clit, circling it firmly, and we stayed that way until Nick returned and crawled back to his former position. Submerged, that's the best way to describe how I felt as Nick's long fingers began to pull at my nipple while James finger-fucked me slowly with his own plan in mind.

"Please," I panted, James's hard cock pushing against my thigh.

"Do you want me to fuck you now?"

"Yes," I spat impatiently.

He leaned in and pulled my lips between his, the lust becoming almost unbearable as he sucked.

"James, please," I pleaded as soon as

I could.

I could feel the smile on his mouth as his one hand lifted my heavy thigh before he expertly drove his hard shaft inside me. He was thicker than Nick, making me feel deliciously full when he finally started moving. James was staring into my eyes again, his gaze unwavering as he fucked me mercifully with the strong roll of his hips.

I could feel his fingertips digging into the base of my neck and the hair on his thighs scrape my skin as his hunger deepened.

"You have a sweet little cunt," he whispered as he fucked he harder. "How many of your lovers have told you that, Lucy?"

"None, no one has ever told me," I answered, kissing him until I felt I would lose my breath. Finally I broke away and Nick took my place as he leaned over me and gave James a long and graceful kiss just inches from my face. I wanted to pull them to me, I wanted to share that moment, their tongues slipping against each other in a familiar sensuousness that made me jealous.

James broke away first and came back to me, sliding his tongue into my open mouth as Nicholas watched from above. I could feel the smile on my friend's face, I didn't have to look, and I knew he was experiencing the same thing I had a moment ago.

James groaned when I ran my hand down his back and sweetly slapped the firm cheek I found beneath it.

"Fuck me harder," I commanded, wondering what he would do.

"Beg me, beg me to fuck you," he ground out, his fingers splaying themselves up the back of my head until he had a fistful of hair, jerking my head back.

I gasped as he slammed into me once, twice, but then stopped. My body immediately began to ache, my hips pushing forward to spur him back into action.

"No," he whispered against my mouth. "You have to beg if you want me to continue."

Just the words pushed me closer to orgasm. This was what I truly wanted. I wanted to be owned, commanded, made to submit to another's desire just by a few spoken words.

"Please, James, please fuck me," I whispered, hoping Nick couldn't fully hear my pleas.

James pushed into me again. "Good,

but you can do better. Can't she, Nick?"

My friend's chuckle rumbled through my torso, his voice sweet and kind when it met my ears. "Just tell him or you will never get what you want," came the sage advice.

"I want you to fuck me," I bit out as I stared directly into his eyes. "Please, fuck me, I need you to, please," I whimpered, licking his thick lips.

"Better," he spat assertively, his hips going back into action as he kissed me again.

There was no time for thought, no time for consideration. I let him fuck me with impunity for what seemed like forever. I was there with him in my entirety as I came, my body shaking against his before I retreated into Nick, who was now hard again. James still held fast a thick mass of hair, allowing him to rein me back in, his lips soothing mine before he withdrew.

"Get me a condom," came the rasp directed past me.

Nicholas didn't hesitate and soon the foil was torn with James properly sheathed and back inside me. After only a few minutes he pulled me hard against him and rolled us over until I was seated properly on top.

"This is how I want to come; make me come," he whispered, pounding into me.

I put both my hands on his chest and began to roll my hips. "Like this?" I asked, knowing full well he had relinquished a little control back my way.

"Yes, just like that," he groaned, his eyes never leaving mine.

This is where I excelled. I liked being on top with other men and I could make them come with just the rhythm of my thick hips, but this was different. James wasn't just some one-night conquest or an insignificant boyfriend, he was someone I had come to truly care about over the past year. Moments later his eyes closed, his hands on my hips, guiding them back and forth across his groin as I worked him closer to completion.

When his fingertips dug in, I knew he was about to orgasm. His eyes flew open a moment later as he ran his hands up my sides before pulling me tight against him.

His head was tucked against mine as he delivered the final thrust and a small curse burrowed into my ear followed by a heavy sigh as his body relaxed.

I nuzzled his neck, gracing it with one long last suck on his salty skin.

"Was that to your satisfaction?" I teased.

James scraped his cheek along mine before finding my lips with his. "Yes, very much." He had answered so softly I could barely hear him. As I rolled off, I found myself face-to-face with Nicholas again.

"You look like you've had enough cock for once," he laughed as his fingers teased the nipple on my tender breast.

"There is no such thing, love," I answered without hesitation before I tucked into his chest and the deep sleep that followed.

Chapter 4

When I awoke in the morning I was alone. James and Nicholas had roused me briefly before they left in the early hours with kisses and promises of meeting at the cafe around noon. The bed felt empty when they withdrew, the sheets cooling rapidly around me, but it wasn't long before I fell back into a deep sleep.

The clock read 11:13 when I walked into the kitchen, reminding me of the date I had made with Nick and James. The adrenaline surged; I had less than an hour to get ready, but the pang in my groin distracted me. I remembered hungrily the lust James had breathed across my lips over and over again, making me immediately ache for him. He had been so intense, but with Nicholas it had been different. The thought of what we had finally done pulled me in two different emotional directions at once. Our friendship could weather anything, of that I was certain, but still I couldn't run from those long ago emotions that were pushing their way inside my head as my fingers fumbled with the clasp of the coffee container.

They were going to be hard to forget.

I was mostly sure we three could return to our former ways, but there was a part of me that pushed the thought away with a thick distaste in my mouth. I wanted them both again, that was for sure, but James, he was the one I wanted the most. I had fucked a lot of men, and for a gay man with no previous training on how to touch a woman, James did a masterful job. I craved his thick fingers on my clit, my cunt clenching as I recalled those soft words of calculated power as he more than fucked me. He had given me a taste of what I really wanted.

I threw the grounds in the press followed by the hot water before I hurried into the bathroom. I needed more than hot water in a French press on the counter. I needed it running over my sins, I needed to think, and the best place for me to do that was always in a hot shower.

What were my sins anyway? Nothing of real consequence—well, except for that one guy, but it certainly wasn't my fault he had failed to mention he was married before I screwed him blind on my living room floor a few years back. No, there was really nothing, except for my sexual exploits, which few were aware of.

I felt the shower turn tepid after a few minutes, and cursed the landlord for the millionth time for installing a tiny water heater that was supposed to supply an entire apartment building. It didn't matter anyway; I needed to get dressed and leave in the next fifteen minutes if I wanted to be on time. I threw on a robe and went back out to the kitchen. The plunger felt sticky under my palm as I pushed it slowly to the bottom, watching the tiny bubbles rise to the surface of my favorite drug. After pouring a cup, I leaned back against the counter and took one long sip, the images from last night permeating my mind again. I shook my head and refocused, but I was interrupted by a soft knock at the door.

A picture of my strange neighbor came to mind, my misdirected mail in hand, as he pushed the greasy tuff of hair back away from his eyes. Garrett was sweet, my age, and totally available, but far too normal in a cool hipster type way. Didn't he know I preferred my sex partners basically unattainable? I thought, pulling my robe tighter around me before I went to answer the next round of rapping.

I chastised myself for not checking the peephole when I saw who was actually there waiting.

"James! What are you doing here?" I asked, more surprised than I should have been.

"May I come in?"

"Of course." I stepped to the side, trying to stop myself from mentally undressing him as soon as he was inside the door.

"Sorry to call so early, but I needed to talk to you," he said as his eyes ran the full length of my body.

"It's no problem. Would you like some coffee?"

"Yes, please," he replied, following me closely into the kitchen.

My head felt thick with skeptical promise and doubt. Why had he come here, alone, and why did he need to speak with me?

"What did you need to talk about?" I said, turning and handing the hot mug to him carefully.

He set it down on the counter, but his eyes never left mine. His demeanor had changed since he came into the apartment and I was quickly unnerved as he stepped into my space.

"Lucy, I didn't come here to talk, necessarily. I wanted to give you your other present," he said, running his hand down the side of my face so kindly that I couldn't help but turn my cheek into the gentle caress.

"What other present?" I asked, suppressing the urge to pull his thumb into my mouth and suck.

"Nick told me about your other fantasy."

"I have so many, which one are you referring to?" My nervousness had left and was replaced by something akin to exhilaration, but I was hesitant.

The corners of his eyes lifted. "You know which one, Lucy. I gave you a little taste last night. Did you like it?" His hand was now on the lapel of my robe, moving up and down as if it was already stroking my clit and making me swell.

"What did my oldest and dearest friend tell you, exactly?"

"He told me you have always wanted a man to dominate you, but not unkindly. No whips or spankings or ropes, just with words—and his cock of course," James added with a smile.

I felt the flush burn through my skin and was sure that he could see it too. I had the fleeting thought of finding Nick and giving him the beating of his life, but it was short lived.

"That's not entirely correct," I said, sounding much braver than I was feeling.

"Well, then why don't you tell me what is. I wouldn't want to give you a present you didn't like."

By now, James had pulled the side of the robe open enough to expose one breast, the nipple already hard.

I took one last brave step, ending up just inches from his face. "Before I tell you anything, does Nick know you're here? We're supposed to meet in twenty minutes," I said, glancing at the clock.

James leaned forward and kissed me. "He is aware and has given me his full permission. I believe he said he wanted to give you exactly what you wanted for your birthday, and this is the icing on the cake."

"Really? Nick knows you are here and about to fuck me again?" I couldn't tell if he was lying, but the wetness running down my thighs didn't care if he was. I already knew what he was here to do and I knew I was going to let him do it.

"He does, and would you like me to? Fuck you again, that is," he said, unconcerned as his thick fingers pulled at my exposed nipple.

"Yes," I whispered, wanting to be on my knees in front of him sucking that beautiful thick cock.

"I know," he murmured as he tugged the robe away, leaving me naked and shameless in the middle of my own kitchen. "Get on your knees, Lucy," he ordered, as if he already knew what I was thinking. "Nick said your favorite thing was a hard cock in your mouth and I want you to show me how much you like it."

I immediately obeyed, watching the smile spread across his lips as my hands unbuttoned his black jeans. The tile was cold and glassy against my shins when I knelt, but it felt good—the impersonal colliding with the sacred.

James made no attempt to help and gave no further instructions as I pulled his already hard cock from its confines. He was cut, thick, and not overly long, which was the ideal combination in my opinion. We fit perfectly together last night, his girth filling the tight wet space between my thighs until I came with none of the usual help by my own hand.

I couldn't resist watching his face as my tongue ran around the pink head between my lips. His mouth was partly open and his eyes locked onto mine as I began the slow, sensuous devotion that made me want to grind my cunt against my own heel. I had found the proper term "cock worship" on the internet a long time ago. Although I thought the terminology strange at the time, it had proved accurate.

Again his fingers trailed down the side of my face as I drew him in and out, pausing only to bite down the sensitive head to watch his eyes slowly shut.

"So good," he whimpered, licking and biting down on his own bottom lip.

He was gorgeous to watch, every reaction sexy and full of desire; James was the male I had been looking for, if only he wasn't in love with my best friend.

I hadn't used my hands yet, wanting

to give him the full range of attention that I had perfected over the years, but my normal patience was thin. I wrapped my hand around the base of his cock, squeezing as I drew him the entire way into my mouth and began to move.

After a minute, his hands went to either side of my head and stilled me. "Fuck, Lucy, you look so hot sucking cock," he panted as his eyes narrowed. Slowly he pushed deeper into my mouth and then withdrew with the same expert control. It was in that moment I saw the shadow cross his face, his demeanor returning to its original intent as he stepped back.

"It's time to move on," he stated in a hard voice.

I rose, unsure of what he meant, my legs unsteady from the promise on his dark features.

"Go over to your beloved sofa, sit down with your ass on the edge, and spread your legs for me."

I must have looked strange, because a small laugh issued from him as he cupped my face in his hands.

"Nicholas told me you were waiting for the right man to help you break it in, and so here I am."

Chapter 5

Moments later I found myself sitting on the couch, spread wide and watching as James removed his shirt before kneeling in front of me. He ran his fingers through the thick flesh atop my legs, his stubbly cheek brushing up the inside of my thigh, making me jump as he neared my cunt.

"It's my time to reciprocate," he

mumbled before taking one long lick up the length of my soaking wet slit. I must have jerked hard because he stopped and looked up at me in annoyance.

"Grab ahold of the couch and don't let go," he ordered, biting the soft skin at the junction of my thigh.

I wrapped my fingers over the edge of the cushion, the tips digging in as James began the long slow pulls on my clit. My back arched unintentionally as the sensations built, my brain somewhere between disbelief and orgasm. No man had ever sucked my pussy with such attention and expertise, especially no one like James. He never stopped moving, his tongue caressing the underside of my clit with sweet short strokes before running the tip just under the hood. It was excruciating. All I wanted to do was come, but I needed this to last as long as it could. There was only this one time— this one morning with him alone—and I was going to do everything I could to keep him between my thighs for as long as possible.

My legs started shaking uncontrollably as he worked me out. His hands left their place on my ass, fingernails scraping the outside of my thighs and back to their original position. Over and over he stroked me, until finally he grasped my knees and opened me to the point of pain. I looked down at the raven black crown of hair between my legs and groaned. James was watching me intently, his lips pulling my clit so sweetly that I came without another second of hesitation. As soon as the first wave rolled, James stopped, allowing me to ride it out, but he never let go. The pleasure was so intense that it was almost painful. It felt like forever until I came down with James nuzzling me softly, his tongue slipping between the soft outer lips of my cunt.

He took his time coming back to me, his mouth wiping the remnants of my orgasm on my thighs, belly, and breasts before he kissed me.

I can honestly say it was the best I'd ever had. He owned me now and we both knew it.

As James rose he pulled me up with him, but his mouth stayed on mine. The soft little moans he issued when my tongue found his made my stomach flutter.

"Lucy," he groaned into my mouth. "Turn around and kneel on the couch."

Again I didn't hesitate. The first thing I saw was the dark red spot where I'd been sitting, my essence soaked into the luxurious fabric, rendering it black. I hoped it would stay.

I grasped the back of the couch and leaned forward, giving James a perfect view of my prostrating ass. I could hear the fabric fold down his long legs as he removed his jeans, the scuff of his feet as he moved towards me.

I glanced around just as his hands grasped my hips. "You are so beautiful," he groaned as his cock ran the length of my slit. It made me shudder.

"Are you ready?" came the question before he slipped the head of his cock inside me.

"Yes, very," I whimpered wanting nothing more than this moment.

I felt the heat of his skin before he laid his chest down on my back, his one hand running over my shoulder before gently encircling the base of my throat.

Pushing into me a little more, he asked, "Do you know the first thing I thought about when I woke up this morning?"

"No, what?" I replied impatiently, wanting him to stop pissing around and fuck me instead.

"I thought about last night and how wet you were when I ran my fingers over your cunt. How I wanted to be back inside you again," he said, pushing the entire way inside me. "Is that better?"

"Jesus, yes, please," I begged, thrusting my full weight back against him.

He pulled back with a chuckle, bringing me with him, his fingers splaying upwards underneath the jut of my chin. Slowly and methodically he fucked me, the slap of his balls on my ass making me want to scream. His other hand came round and held on to my breast just as his mouth bit down on the back of my neck, the scrape of teeth on flesh. I felt completely possessed for the first time in my life and it scared me.

James licked at the marks he'd left on my skin, his breath hot as he slammed into me harder.

"Do you know how fucking hot you are, Lucy? The first time I met you I wanted to fuck you," he said as he pulled my head around to kiss me.

"Harder, fuck me harder," I demanded against his mouth, not knowing how else to respond to such a confession.

"Like this?" He slammed into me so hard it pushed me against the back of the couch, my nipples scraping across the soft velvet, making me whimper.

To my disappointment, his hand left my throat and found its way down to my clit. "I want you to come again," he whispered in my ear.

Slowly he rubbed me from the front as his cock filled me from the back. It only took a minute before the next orgasm came bearing down, making me cry out.

"Good girl, such a good girl," was the only thing he said as my body shook against his. I could hardly catch my breath, but James pulled out and retrieved a condom from his jeans, letting me come down alone. I looked back and watched him roll the rubber on, his eyes glazed over.

"Get up and bend over the end of

the couch, Lucy," he said and extended his hand.

My legs almost failed when my feet hit the floor, but James pulled me against him, taking my lips before I had the chance to embarrass myself.

I broke anyway and did as told, wondering if I would ever find someone like him to be my full time lover. I had tried. Over the years, I had held auditions that would have left even a Hollywood producer in envy of my efforts, but never had anyone overtaken me like James just had. A wave of resentment went through me. Nicholas had it all, he always did. He was handsome, smart, and sexy, and he had the boyfriend that I now coveted.

James interrupted my thought, turning me around and laying one hand between my shoulder blades as he put me where he wanted.

The sides of the couch were high, the arm rolled smooth and clean away from the deep cushions below, and now that I was bent over, my feet barely touched the floor.

James took his time, kneading my ass cheeks for a moment before he spread them apart. I felt the tip of his cock push easily between my drenched outer lips until he sunk the whole way in with one forceful thrust. It felt so good to be so full.

The moments passed and his speed increased until, finally, he ran his hands underneath my waist and pulled me tight against him. To my pleasure, his one hand went to the base of my throat again and his mouth sucked at the nape of my neck, spurring me to the next release.

"I'm not going to last much longer," he whispered in my ear. "I want you to come again before I do," he commanded as his free hand came around to find my clit with efficiency.

I reached back and ran my hand up the side of his face before I wrapped my fingers around the short hairs at the nape of his neck. He grunted as I pulled hard, wanting to inflict a little pain of my own, but it spurred a retaliation that made me come for the final time.

James bit down on my neck again, teeth bruising my skin, pounding inside me until I screamed.

"That's it," he growled. "Come all over my cock, I love how it feels."

That was all it took. My legs gave way as my cunt gripped him, my upper body slipping against his chest. There were words coming out of my mouth but they made no sense.

"Yes, yes, good girl," he said, pushing me forward until my face hit the cushion.

James gave one last low growl and came, punctuating his release with a series of hard thrusts before I felt his body ease. He gave my ass one last slap and pulled out, his breathing labored.

"Come here," he said, running his hand down the length of my spine.

I struggled a moment, weak from the pleasure I'd just endured. As I righted myself, James pulled me round and into him.

"That was amazing," he whispered, kissing me hard. I could feel his still half hard cock against my belly, spurring me to pull off the condom and begin stroking him softly.

His groan filled my mouth. "That was the best present I ever got. Thank you."

"It was my pleasure. You can thank Nick. He was the one who suggested it."

"Was he?" I pulled away, not believing it was Nick's idea.

James smiled and ran his fingers between my breasts. "It was. You can ask him yourself."

"Oh, I will, to be sure." I grabbed his hand and brought it to my mouth and began sucking on his index finger.

James closed his eyes, his head loose on his neck. "Haven't you had enough?"

"Never," came my one word reply.

"Nick said you were insatiable." He opened his eyes and watched as I drew him between my lips, my tongue stroking the underside as I imagined it was his stiff cock between my lips again.

"I've missed this," he murmured to himself.

Slowly I stopped, wondering what he meant. "Missed what?"

"Nothing," he said quickly, pulling his hand away.

"What's wrong?" I asked, coming against him.

"Nothing, Lucy, I just got lost in the moment." He kissed me with sweetness just as his phone went off.

I felt the smile form on his lips before he pulled away to answer it.

"We're almost ready, should be there in twenty," he told the person on the phone, glancing back at me with a sly grin. He paused a minute before laughing. "No, she looks satiated, but I'll let her be the one to tell you."

My mouth popped open, knowing

full well who he was talking to, but the conversation was over before I got to utter one of my well-known biting retorts.

"Guess we should put on some clothes," James said, coming over and cupping my face as one last kiss was issued.

"That would be appropriate," I said, turning away towards the bedroom, suddenly needing a space between us; the thought of seeing Nicholas made my heart accelerate. Obviously he had condoned this as per their conversation on the phone, but the question of why was making me feel unbalanced. He was giving to a fault where I was concerned, but this seemed over the line, even for him.

I threw on my Sunday dress; old, soft, and blue, the neckline wide, making wearing a bra with it impossible. I'd had it a long time. Nick had helped me pick it out the summer we became friends. I wore it often when we went out for coffee on the weekends and it had had been dubbed by Nick as my 'Sunday best,' always making him smile when he saw me wear it. It seemed relevant in the moment I put it on, but as James and I walked out the door I felt the slightest pang of remorse.

Chapter 6

Nicholas was already seated with one empty coffee cup to his left and another full one in front of him. He rose in greeting when he saw us approach, his tight peach t-shirt the perfect color against the healthy glow of his skin.

His smile was so brilliant that the pang of remorse felt more like a wave and I was glad James was beside me, even if his silent support was unknown to anyone but myself.

Nick hugged me thoroughly and skimmed a finger across the open neckline of the dress.

"She doesn't look too overtired," Nick commented as he leaned into and past me to give his lover a kiss before his soft lips met mine.

"I believe Lucy is no worse for wear," James retorted. He pulled out the chair next to Nick's and motioned for me to sit.

"I also believe I am standing right here and am fully well aware of the state of my own being."

Nicholas laughed. "Of course you are. Thanks for wearing the dress," he said as the waiter came over to take our order.

I sat and looked between them, watching as they shared a knowing look.

"So," Nick began, settling back in

his seat. "Did you enjoy the rest of your birthday present?" He took a sip of his coffee.

"Yes, very much so. It was quite a surprise."

Another ear-to-ear grin graced his face. "I'm glad you enjoyed it. James is quite adept at many things."

"Adept?" James echoed, removing a pack of cigarettes from the front pocket of his jeans. "That's the first time I've heard it called that."

Nick rolled his eyes. "You know what I mean."

"Do you mind?" James asked, looking at me.

"No, but I didn't know you smoked."

"I do every now and then, it's a remnant from my past life." He lit the cigarette and took a deep drag, the blue and white smoke illuminated by the sunlight on its expulsion.

As I watched him smoke, my nervousness dissipated. They were both so relaxed and seemingly unfazed by what we had all shared, it would be a shame for me to be the only one with reservations.

The waiter brought over the coffees, giving James a long look as he retreated towards another table.

"I see your fan base is quite large," I joked.

Nick snorted in agreement. "Larger than you know."

"What's that supposed to mean?" I asked, feeling the warmth of the coffee and midday sun easing me back into myself. My eye caught that of a thick, older, dark haired man sitting alone two tables away. The corner of his mouth drew up in a lazy smile as he skimmed over the thin material that clearly gave up my unrestrained breasts.

As my mind wondered— it always did when I saw something of potential—I heard Nick clear his throat.

"What it means is that James really does have a past life."

"Sorry?" I said distracted. "What past life? Were you in the circus or something? the CIA?"

James laughed. "No, but I think you'll be surprised."

"I don't think I could be any more surprised than I have been in the past twenty-four hours, but you can certainly try."

"James used to be married," Nick announced, the tone of his voice completely free of mirth or sarcasm for once.

"Really? That's not that surprising," I said, and I gave Nick's leg a shove with mine under the table. "What was his name?"

"Her name, you mean," James said, watching me closely.

"*Her* name? A woman? You were married to a woman?"

"See, you are surprised," James said, squinting through a long exhale of sooty air.

"Well, yes, I am," I stuttered, making them both smile. "How long were you married?"

"Five painful years," he replied with sadness in his voice. "She was young, or should I say, we were young. It was a long time ago."

I watched as he leaned to the side and stubbed the smoke out on the ground, my mind full of questions.

"Did you know back then you were gay, or was this more of a recent development?" I asked quietly.

"James isn't exactly gay," Nick

chimed in as he leaned forward into the conversation. "I believe the correct term is bisexual."

"Christ, Nick, I know what the correct term is." I was slightly annoyed that I had been left out of such pertinent information about the man I had just fucked so utterly and completely without hesitation.

"So," I said, turning back to James, "you just like to relive a little of your old life now and then, is that it?"

"Lucy," Nick said in that exasperated tone I hated so much, "I know what you're thinking and I want you to stop. It's not like that at all."

"Well, what the fuck is it like then, Nick?"

"It's like we told you, we wanted to give you something special for your birthday. We both wanted to be with you, even if we didn't say that outright last night."

I could feel the anger building, but I knew it was unwarranted. Nicholas always told me the truth even if I didn't want to hear it, and now, like always, he was being honest to a fault.

Pushing myself into the seat of the chair as hard as I could, I looked back and forth between them, old and new feelings pummeling me and threatening to ruin the best birthday I'd ever had.

James reached out and took my hand. "Lucy, we would never take advantage of you. We both love you, you know that?"

"Yes, of course I do. That's not the problem."

"What is the problem then? The last thing Nick and I would want is to upset you. We just want you to be happy."

He said it with such genuine warmth

and compassion that I became brave, really brave, for the first time in my life. The desire I had for Nicholas so long ago had returned and the overwhelming craving I had for James made my body ache. I was perfectly placed between my happy, wasn't I? It was purely on instinct, what came next. I knew what I wanted and the rest would sort itself out later.

I turned, leaned in, and gave my best friend a kiss that could in no way be mistaken. As I broke away, I saw the dark haired man smirk, relishing the surprise of a girl kissing an obviously gay man.

Nick's face softened, his eyes hooded as he came into the moment. "Oh," he said quietly, very much understanding what I was getting at. I rose and put a twenty on the table.

"I'm going home if you both want to come with me. Your choice," I said, giving the stranger a nod and a smile as I walked away.

The sound of two chairs being pushed back on the cement was all the confirmation I could have hoped for.

In the short time it took us to get to my apartment there was no conversation or discussion about what was about to happen, but I could feel the energy building as we neared the fourth floor landing. As I slipped the key in the lock, I felt a hand at the base of my neck. It was Nick.

"This is what you want?"

I turned and looked back at him. "It is, and if you don't, I will totally understand." I glanced over at James. "And that goes for you as well," I said.

Nick leaned in and began sucking and biting at my lips. "I think we are all agreed. Yes, James?"

"Quite agreed," he said, tucking into the back of his lover and giving me *that look*, the one that made my stomach drop.

I could hear the *Pretty Lights* mix James had made me last month playing on the alarm clock in my bedroom as we came through the door, my favorite song just beginning as the lock clicked shut. A second later I had Nick's t-shirt over his head while James unbuttoned his lover's jeans from behind. Nick's hands were at my breasts, thumbs circling the stiff nipples that protruded beneath the thin fabric.

"I've thought of this more than once," he whispered as I stroked his cock through the stiff denim.

"What have you thought, love?" I begged.

I swear he blushed before the answer left his lips. "This, Lucy, the three of us together."

All my words were lost, my head nodding as the corners of my mouth rose. I didn't care that it wasn't forever, didn't care that it made me more afraid than anything I'd ever felt, all I wanted was them.

I kissed Nick slowly, wanting to savor this moment of truth, summoning the courage to ask for what I wanted next.

"Will you both?" I whispered finally.

"Both what?" James prompted, knowing full well what I wanted.

Nick pulled the dress from my shoulders to expose my upper body. "You want us both to fuck you," he said, cupping each breast in turn.

"I want you to fuck me at the same time," I spit out hungrily.

"We know," they answered in unison.

I let James guide us towards the couch, the anticipation running down the inside of my thighs with the knowledge I was getting exactly what I wanted. James sat down and pulled me onto his lap so that I was facing him. He had already removed his shirt but still had his jeans on and I could feel the hardness beneath rubbing against my swollen cunt. I could already feel him inside me.

Nick removed the rest of his clothes and came up behind me. His hand ran down between my thighs, finding my clit with ease; he began to stroke. "We should move to the bedroom," he mumbled as I panted across James's cheek.

"No, we're taking her on this couch," James said wickedly, thrusting up against my swollen cunt. "You want it here, don't you? You want to christen it again with two cocks inside you."

"Yes, I want you to fuck me here," I demanded as my lips came down onto his.

It only took another few minutes before James had me begging again. He was efficient in his vocal advocation of my desires, we three naked with James beneath me as Nick rimmed my ass. James had one hand dug into the hair on top of my head, holding me in place while his cock slipped back and forth across my clit.

"You want me to fuck you now?" he asked, slapping my ass with the other hand.

"Yes, I want you to fuck me. Please fuck me," I begged to his satisfaction.

I felt the head of his cock at the opening of my cunt, but I didn't move. It was all I could do not to push my hips down and back to sheath him inside me, my overwhelming greed threatening to make me disobey him.

Slowly, his tongue filled my mouth and retreated. Over and over he fucked my mouth but not my cunt, making me whimper in anticipation.

He pulled back, smiling. "Are you ready to fill that beautiful ass of hers yet, Nick?" he asked, pushing his cock inside me just a little as a tease.

I heard the foil rip and then Nick's hard shaft ran between my ass cheeks. "I think we're both ready," he breathed, pushing the tip of his cock inside me.

I flinched, but it was a good pain amplified by the one who was inflicting it. I cried out as James suddenly pushed the entire way inside me and slowly started moving. "Is that better, love?" he whispered.

"Much better," I said, pulling his bottom lip between my teeth.

Nick's fingertips dug painfully into the fleshiness of my hips, his restraint evident from the noises he was making.

I knew he was hesitating and I knew why. Slowly, I pushed myself back against him, taking that long cock completely inside me as James whispered praise into my ear.

"Such a good girl. Do you like that beautiful cock in your ass? Feels good, doesn't it?"

In that moment, I knew exactly what Nick felt last night. "I love it, I love feeling you both inside me," I said, licking his mouth.

Nick bent forward, his hot skin on my back, his breathing rapid on the nape of my neck as he began to move.

My heart ached. I'd never felt so full.

THE END

ABOUT THE AUTHOR

Lilith Wes is a photographer and writer. She lives
with her husband, daughter, and orange cat on the
East Coast.

We Love Lucy
is available as an enhanced ebook
with additional multimedia content for
Apple iBooks and Amazon Kindle.

For more information, visit
www.badlandsunlimited.com